Boots
for Beth

Boots
for Beth

Alex Moran

**Illustrated by
Lisa Campbell Ernst**

Green Light Readers
Harcourt, Inc.

Orlando Austin New York San Diego Toronto London

Beth was sad.

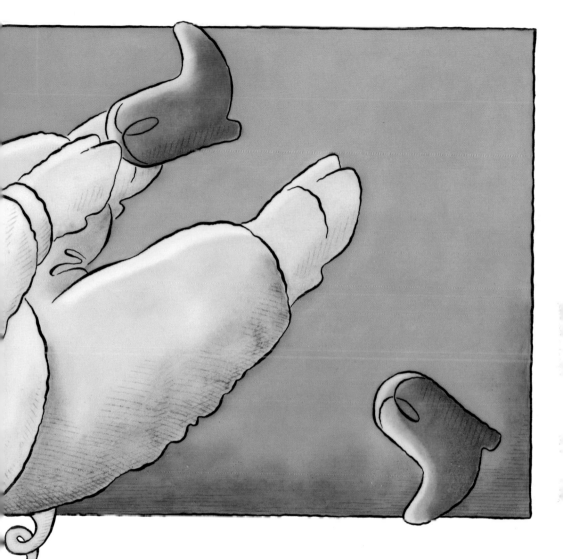

"My red boots don't fit," she cried.
"I cannot get them on."

"Could you use my boots?" asked Meg.

"Too big," said Beth.

"Will my boots fit?" asked Ned.

"Too small," said Beth.

"Could you use my boots?" asked Liz.

"Too soft," said Beth.

"Will my boots help?" asked Ted.

"Too wet," said Beth.

"Can you put on my boot?" asked Jeff.

"Too thin," said Beth.

Beth still felt sad.
Her friends all felt bad.

Then they found a
big surprise for Beth.

"New red boots," said Beth.
"Thanks!"

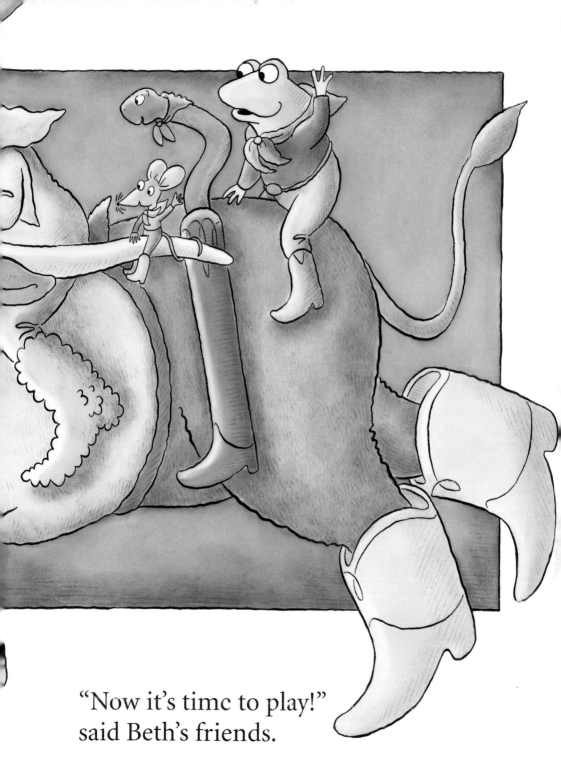

"Now it's time to play!"
said Beth's friends.

Think About It

1. What problem does Beth have?

2. How is Beth's problem solved?

3. What happens first in the story? What happens last?

4. How can you tell that Beth's friends are nice?

5. Have you ever had a problem like Beth's? What did you do?

Shoes Around the World

paper   **crayons or markers**

1. Draw a picture of your favorite shoes.

2. Look at pictures of people who live around the world. Draw pictures of what they wear on their feet.

Who wears shoes that look like yours?

Meet the Illustrator

Lisa Campbell Ernst got the idea for *Boots for Beth* while shopping for shoes with her two children. "How sad we feel when a favorite pair of shoes no longer fits," she says. "Then the search for just the right new pair begins. Some shoes are too big, too small, too stiff. At last you find just the right ones!"

Lisa Campbell Ernst

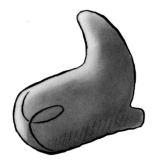